THINK LIKE A GOAT?

by

Allison Mitcham and Stephanie Mitcham

illustrated by

Naomi Mitcham and Peter Mitcham

Sumner, Iowa, USA

ISBN 0-9664476-3-8

Published 2005, Crane Creek Publications

My Aunt Abby has just said, "Jason, you'd better learn to think like a goat."
I'm shocked.

I'm shocked is one of my grandmother's expressions. I haven't had a chance to use it before, but I like the sound of it coming from me - even if I only say it under my breath.

Anyhow, Aunt Abby sounds serious. How could she be?

Why would *I* want to think like a goat? Why would ANYONE?

Already, after that big billy tried to butt me, and did butt Uncle John, I want to steer clear of these critters. But Aunt Abby says I need to think about why these things happened.

"Maybe," she said, "the Boer billy didn't like the way you were acting ... or the way Uncle John was behaving either. Do you remember what you were doing when the billy tried to butt you and Uncle John?"

"All I was doing was practising my karate kicks."

"And where were you doing that?"

"Didn't you see me? I was just outside his pen."

"Do you think the Boer billy minded you doing this?"

"How would I know?"

"Maybe you frightened him or put him in a bad mood because he thought you were showing off."

"And what was Uncle John doing when he got butted?"

"Oh, I don't know. Just trying to move the Angora billy out onto pasture. He needed to get the billy out of there, didn't he?"

"Yes, but maybe not like that."

"Why not?"

"Well, don't you think he might have been a bit rough?

"If you don't want the Angora billies or the Boer billy in the next pen to butt you, you'd better be careful how you act around them. Think about how they'll feel if you frighten them. Maybe you should imagine yourself in their place. Perhaps then neither you nor the billies will get stressed out - or hurt. Wouldn't that be a good reason for learning to think like a goat?"

That's three times already Aunt Abby has told me I should think like a goat. I'm getting tired of hearing this same thing. Three times in one afternoon - my first afternoon here - is too much.

None of Aunt Abby's animals look to me as if they're thinking about anything right now! Well, except for the donkey.

I've never heard anyone say anything so silly. I'm eight years old already and I've heard a lot of dumb stuff in my time. But this trying to think like a goat has to be the most ridiculous.

I like that word: *ridiculous* is really my Grammy's word. I'm just borrowing it. It seems to me that people like Grammy own some words. I wonder.

My mom and dad often tell me not to say or do silly things. But nobody ever suggests that Aunt Abby does or says things that don't make sense. Everyone says she's REALLY, REALLY smart and REALLY, REALLY thoughtful - even Grampa, who knows a lot and who says funny things that make us all laugh.

But Grampa tells me he doesn't like foolishness.

"Listen to your Aunt Abby," Grampa says. "Figure out what she means. She's a veterinarian - a good one - who can mostly tell what an animal is thinking. Seeing as how animals can't talk, that's important. Even with people, you often can't tell what they're thinking unless you watch how they act.... Watch carefully."

So I'm pretty mixed up right now. And not too happy. This was supposed to be a fun time.

Two whole weeks of fun on the farm, my mom said when she dropped me off to visit this aunt I've never seen before.

Like my mom, this aunt is very pretty, though they don't look a lot alike. My mom has long blond hair and blue eyes. My aunt has long dark hair and brown eyes. They're as different to look at as my aunt's two Labradors who are brothers.

Nibby is pale yellow. Niblet is his full name because he's corn-colored. Schwartz is black. My aunt says his name means *black* in German. Both dogs are beautiful and good-tempered. I could tell that right away.

When I told Aunt Abby that I liked her Labradors and thought they liked me, she said she guessed I was right.

Then she said, "If you're pretty sure what Nibby and Schwartz are thinking, that's a start. Now you just have to watch the farm animals in the same way. I think you'll find that Big Red, the Boer who came from Texas, Sammie, the Savanna billy, and all the Angoras are as different from one another and from the dogs as people are different from each other. So you have to watch carefully to tell what's on their minds."

***

Last night I dreamed of goats - goats doing all sorts of far out antics, particularly climbing. *Antics* is another of Grammy's words I like.

It's funny seeing goats climb. Some of them climb more than others, but the ones that get up on tree branches look as if they're having fun. I can't figure out why they don't fall. They don't have claws like a cat or fingers like me. Anyway, they seem to know what they're doing.

Goats are like me in wanting to climb. I just LOVE to climb.

Anyway, the goats in my dream were high climbers - really HIGH climbers. They were as different from Aunt Abby's real goats, which keep to low branches, as circus trapeze acrobats are from me.

Aunt Abby said I was laughing in my sleep, so I suppose that was because I liked my dream so much.

***

Now that I've been here a whole week I quite like a lot of the things I've been doing.

It's nice in the early morning to help Uncle John fill the bird feeders before he goes to work. Neither of us can understand why those birds are such messy eaters. They drop half the seeds we feed them onto the deck.

Anyhow, I like to watch them for a while, but not for as long as Uncle John's favorite cat. Mama Toes watches those birds for hours.

I also like to help Aunt Abby and Colin with the chores. Sometimes.

When Colin lets the border collies out they go crazy. They tear back and forth across the yard. I've never seen dogs move as fast as these two.

And when Aunt Abby puts them to work rounding up the goats and sheep in the pasture it's really fun to be there. It's amazing! Better than watching T.V.

Aunt Abby says her goats and sheep are *dog broken* by now. That means they mostly know what Jen and Flo want them to do.

When Aunt Abby saw how impressed I was with her collies, she agreed that Jen and Flo are great helpers. And she said to me, "Do you notice how they work quietly and without being rough?"

That is true. As I said before, they are amazing.

This afternoon, though, I am bored. Aunt Abby is busy with visitors from far away. They want to buy some of her goats or sheep, so right now she has no time for me.

She told me to be good, to find something sensible to do until these people leave. I'm not sure what Aunt Abby had in mind when she told me to do *something sensible*.

What I want to do is play, but there is no one to play with except Nibby and Schwartz, and they're asleep after their long pasture run. They are tired out after chasing each other and retrieving all the sticks I threw into the creek for them. I was running too, but I'm not tired.

None of the animals seems very lively right now.

The sheep are hardly moving in the upper pasture. Some of them are eating grass and some are lying down.

The goats are at the edge of the woods. A few of them are browsing. A lot of them are resting. Maybe they're bored too. I wonder.

Even Miss Annie Tolie - Annie for short - the Anatolian shepherd dog, whose job is to watch over the sheep and goats and make sure no dangerous creatures attack them, is sound asleep. She must be worn out because she stays up all night guarding *her* animals. Nighttime is when she goes after anything she finds strange.

Last night she tore the towels off the clothesline. Aunt Abby had forgotten to bring them in, and I guess Annie figured they shouldn't be out there dancing around in the moonlight. I suppose they looked strange to her.

***

I am still thinking about Annie and the clothes when all of a sudden I see something moving fast along the fence. At first I think it's a very big dog. Then I remember pictures in my nature books and on T.V. This creature looks a lot like a wolf - except he is smaller. He keeps looking over his shoulder as if he thinks there might be someone following him.

I am frightened. He moves so fast - and smoothly. And because it's daytime and she's so tired after being up all night, Annie hasn't noticed this wolf creature.

I tell myself that at least this wild animal is on the other side of the far fence. But what, I wonder could happen if he got through both fences? He can run faster than I can. He seems almost as fast a runner as the border collies. Maybe faster. He moves in a different way though - smoothly, not darting like they do.

I can see Big Red from here. He's in the closest pasture. I think he acts worried. Like me - though I am safer than he is. I am behind two fences, in the yard which is closest to the house.

The sheep are all on their feet now and moving towards me like a big wave. The goats are also on the move. A big nanny seems to have organized the younger, smaller nannies and they are coming towards me and the gate I'm kneeling on.

They have waded through the shallow brook, but Mollie, the donkey, is pawing the ground on the other side. I'd say she wants to deal with what I think she thinks is a strange dog - a bad dog that is going to hurt *her* goats and sheep. But she won't cross the brook.

The water would be only up to her ankles. Besides, she could jump - or even step - across it if she wanted. But she doesn't. Instead, she begins to cry, "Eee-oh, eee-oh." It's a very sad-sounding noise. Then I remember that every single one of my Aunt Abby's donkeys - all four of them - are afraid to walk through water.

Although I know that's a silly fear, I suddenly think that just about everyone's got at least one fear that doesn't make much sense to anyone else.

The lead goat looks around. I can see she's trying to be cool and not let the others see she's worried - concerned because she figures that a dangerous creature is out there. Afraid too because Annie is not there and the guard donkey is not able to protect her flock because of her fear of the water.

This goat who is in charge brings her goats up to the gate and stares at me. I know what she is trying to say.

"So, you want me to open the gate and let you guys into the yard," I say to her out loud.

I'm sure that's what she is telling me. I figure we're all in this together. We're all frightened of the creature I think might be a wolf.

The gate is hard to open. When I take off the chains, the wind still holds it shut. But I push harder and it finally opens. The goats come flooding into the yard. The sheep are not far behind.

I pull the gate to behind them.

The poor donkey is still crying on the other side of the brook.

The border collies know something is up too. They are barking, but they can't get out of their pens.

Aunt Abby comes running out of the house. She looks anxious - and not very pleased.

"What's all the hullabaloo about?" she shouts. "What on earth do you think you're doing?"

I want to cry, but I don't. Not quite. Anyway, I can see that crying isn't going to help anything right now. Besides, I'm relieved to see Aunt Abby, even if she scolds me.

"There's a wolf or something like it out there," I call out in a voice that hardly sounds like mine. "He's after us. Well, after something here. The goats and sheep, I guess."

I can see that Aunt Abby thinks I am making this up, like in the story where the boy keeps calling *wolf, wolf*, and he is only pretending. I am worried because now I can't see the wolflike creature, so I can't show Aunt Abby.

Then, suddenly there he is again. He is about to dig his way under the fence near the brook where the water has washed away some of the earth and given him a start on a hole.

"There he is," I yell, pointing, excited again and not so frightened now that I have a grownup nearby who I think will know how to cope.

Suddenly Aunt Abby sees the wolf creature too. Now she understands the panic the animals and I have been feeling.

She stands still and watches. She is calm.

"He is a coyote," she says finally. "Not a wolf. But a big coyote.

"I'm going to stop him getting into the pasture. You stay here and watch over the goats and sheep. Colin should be along soon to help."

Aunt Abby calls Annie who comes out of the machine shed at a run. They set off towards the fence where the coyote is. Annie is running ahead.

I am frightened for her. She is, I think, very brave - and so is Aunt Abby.

The coyote has stopped digging. He and Aunt Abby are watching each other. Aunt Abby keeps on going. Annie is still ahead.

Annie is a lot bigger than the coyote. Twice as big, I'd say. Still, I wonder how she will deal with this wild animal. She does not seem afraid, though. Maybe she gets her courage partly from Aunt Abby who still doesn't act scared. Then I remember that, according to Aunt Abby, Anatolian shepherds are used to coping with wild animals who threaten the animals they are guarding. Aunt Abby has told me that good Anatolians are famous guardian dogs.

Still, Annie is not very old and, because Aunt Abby says she hasn't encountered wild animals up till now, it's hard to tell how she will react.

Halfway to the far fence, I hear Aunt Abby calling Annie. The dog stops, stares toward the fence and then heads straight for where the coyote was digging. Can she ever run!

The coyote has stopped digging. He puts his head on one side and watches Annie. Then he turns and trots off as if he didn't care about getting into the pasture anyway. A few seconds later he starts to really move. He takes long, easy, swinging strides. He keeps looking back over his shoulder to see, I suppose, if he is being followed.

The last I see of him he has crossed the road onto the open low land by the creek and disappeared into the neighbor's corn field. Now that he is not coming my way, I think he looked beautiful - and smart.

***

Before Aunt Abby goes back to her visitors, she asks Colin if he will fix the fence and stop up the hole, just in case the coyote returns. Then she tells me I am the hero of the day.

She says I knew the right thing to do about opening the gate and letting the goats and sheep into the yard where they'd be safer for the time being. She says she guesses I knew what to do because I've been watching so carefully all week that I have learned to understand those animals.

I feel very proud when she says this, and I am imagining how I will describe this real life adventure to my friend Trevor at home, when Aunt Abby, who is almost at the house, turns round, laughing, and calls out: "So, Jason, I guess now you know how to think like a goat!"

This is true. And I have to laugh every time I think back over all these happenings. I wonder if I'll dream and laugh in my sleep again tonight?